This book belongs to

. . . .

. . . .

CONTENTS

Illustrated by Stuart Trotter
Stories by Stuart Trotter
Text and couplets by Anna Bowles
Edited by Anna Bowles
Designed by Martin Aggett

THE RUPERT ANNUAL

EXPRESS NEWSPAPERS

EGMONT
We bring stories to life

Published in Great Britain 2008 by Egmont UK Limited
239 Kensington High Street, London W8 6SA
Rupert Bear ®, © Entertainment Rights Distribution Limited/Express Newspapers 2008

ISBN 978 1 4052 3890 8
Printed in Italy

No. 73

£7.99

MEET RUPERT AND HIS FRIENDS

If you've been to Nutwood before, you'll know some of these faces.
How many do you recognise?

RUPERT BEAR
Rupert Bear is everyone's best friend. He's always loyal, brave and helpful.

BILL BADGER
Bill is always up for an adventure. He's easy-going, and resourceful too.

EDWARD TRUNK
Edward is very strong, but also gentle and kind. He's a good friend to everyone.

ALGY PUG
Algy is a good friend, but also likes to play tricks on Rupert and the others!

PODGY PIG
Podgy's favourite thing is food, but he remembers that friends are important too.

BINGO PUP
Bingo is a brainbox! He's the one who thinks his way out of trouble.

CLARA CAT
Clara is new to Nutwood. She's small and nimble, which comes in handy!

TIGERLILY
Tigerlily is the daughter of the Chinese Conjuror. She can do magic!

FREDDIE & FERDIE FOX
The naughtiest children in Nutwood! But they aren't really bad, they just don't think about consequences.

REX & REGGIE RABBIT
The Rabbits are Nutwood's other set of twins. They're much better behaved!

GREGORY GUINEAPIG
Gregory is a bit younger than most of the friends. Rupert often ends up rescuing him!

WILLIE MOUSE
Willie is the well-meaning but nervous type, who goes to pieces if there's trouble.

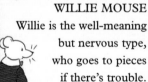

MR & MRS BEAR
Rupert's parents usually prefer to stay at home. But not always!

THE OLD PROFESSOR & BODKIN
The inventor and his assistant live in a tower that is the last remnant of Nutwood Castle.

PC GROWLER
Nutwood's police constable is always on hand to round up any ne'er-do-wells.

WISE OLD GOAT
This mysterious old sage is a member of a mystic order with special powers.

Of course, Rupert has lots of other friends, and is always meeting new ones.
Some of them appear in this book, and some of them appear in earlier stories.
Did you know that Rupert has been having adventures for over 80 years? Find out more on page 49.

RUPERT

and the
Ice-Cream Van

RUPERT WAKES UP TO AN EXCITING DAY

When Rupert wakes it's barely light,
But somehow getting up seems right.

He's out of bed and dressing fast.
It's Nutwood Fair today! At last!

His mum is making something cold.
Ooh – could that be a lolly mould?

Mum tells him it's a special treat,
And says to look out on the street.

One morning, Rupert wakes up early. At first he can't work out why he feels something big is going to happen. Then he realises: it's Nutwood Fair today!

It's particularly exciting, because Dad has been hinting about a mysterious surprise that will make the Fair even more special this year.

Rupert hurries to get into his clothes, then runs downstairs to where Mum is busy in the kitchen. It looks like she's making ice-cream.

"I'm going to the Fair," says Rupert. "Are you and Dad coming?"

"Yes we are – when I've finished," says Mum with a mysterious smile. "Why don't you go outside and see what Dad is doing?"

Rupert rushes out into the spring sunshine. Dad is not in the garden, so Rupert goes down the path to the gate and has a look outside. What he sees makes him gasp with surprise and delight.

RUPERT'S DAD HAS AN ICE-CREAM VAN

An ice-cream van for Nutwood Fair!
It's been restored by Mr Bear.

Inside are freezers, chests and such.
These lights will be a perfect touch.

"I hope they work," says Dad. "You wait;
I'll screw this on the backing plate."

The lights come on, and Rupert cheers.
This Fair will be the best for years!

It's an ice-cream van!

"So you like it?" grins Dad. "I thought you might. It's a vintage model, and it was just sitting in Mr Hippo's garage, so I asked if I could borrow it for Nutwood Fair."

"Does it really go?" asks Rupert excitedly.

"It does now I've spruced it up. I just need to tidy up inside. Can you give me a hand?"

Rupert peers into the old van. Amongst the curious machines for making and storing ice-cream, there is a pair of big fake cornets.

"What are these?" asks Rupert.

"Why, that explains the square patches on the front of the van!" exclaims dad. "These big cones are lights. Help me screw them on to the panels, and we'll see if they still work."

The lights do indeed still work.

"Now it's perfect," says Rupert.

RUPERT HAS AN IDEA

*But dad just frowns and rubs his fur.
"It's lovely, but it lacks – um... er..."*

*"A jingle!" Rupert cries. "That's what!
Let's see what the Professor's got."*

*So Rupert goes and talks to Bill,
And off they run down Nutwood Hill.*

*The Old Professor's on his tower,
Just strolling at this early hour.*

"It does look good," agrees Dad. "But, you know, an ice-cream van normally plays some kind of tune, so people know it's coming."

Rupert understands what he means.

"A jingle! That's what we need. I'm sure the Old Professor would help. Last week he told me all about the recording studio he was building."

"That would be grand," says Dad.

So Rupert runs off towards his old friend's home, which is a tower on the edge of Nutwood. On the way he meets Bill Badger, Edward Trunk and Algy Pug. He tells them the plan, and they soon come up with some instruments. Bill has some horns that came from a Christmas cracker, and Algy has a toy drum.

When they come in sight of the tower, they see the Old Professor taking a morning stroll on the roof. He waves to them, shouts hello, then disappears inside the building.

RUPERT RECORDS A JINGLE

Now Rupert asks the kind old man
To help make music for the van.

They take deep breaths and get stuck in.
Poor Bodkin's thinking: "What a din!"

A music box his old friend had
Lets Rupert tape the tune for dad.

"Great stuff! Now go," says Mr Bear.
"We'll join you later at the Fair."

By the time the friends reach the Professor's door, he is there waiting for them.

"An ice-cream van jingle?" he says when Rupert tells him what they need. "Well, well, we'll see what we can do."

He shows the friends to his experimental recording studio, and flicks the RECORD switch.

Rupert and Algy blow the horns, Bill bangs his drum, and Edward trumpets through his trunk.

"Good heavens!" cries Bodkin, wincing. "You call that music?"

"Beautiful!" smiles the Professor, who is not so easily daunted.

He transfers the recording to a special music box, and gives it to Rupert to take home to Dad.

"This will do the trick," laughs Dad when he listens to the jingle. "It's a real fanfare, all right. Everyone will know we're coming."

RUPERT GOES TO THE FAIR

So Rupert heads off at a run.
The Fair is waiting! Time for fun!

There's stalls and sideshows, games and slides,
And Rupert's favourite fairground rides.

Just hit the coconut to score.
You keep it if it strikes the floor!

Then Rupert tries the carousel,
And Bill and Algy come as well.

Then Rupert runs off to the Fair. Not a moment too soon, as he feels he could burst with excitement!

Nutwood looks very different from its normal peaceful self. The main street is busy with stalls, all filled with toys and sweets and wonderful games. In the distance there's a marquee tent and a slide that's as tall as a house.

The only problem is deciding what to do first! Algy Pug is having a go at the coconut shy. It's a game of skill, where you try to knock a coconut right off its perch by throwing a little ball. If you succeed, you get to keep the coconut and eat it.

This is Algy's favourite kind of game, but he's not having any luck today.

"Come on," says Rupert comfortingly. "You can try again later. Why don't we go on the carousel?"

Bill joins them, and the three friends ride round and round on the handsome painted horses.

THE PROFESSOR IN A BALLOON

Above the roofs of Nutwood town,
An air balloon is coming down.

Between the ropes, two friends peer out.
"We've come to offer rides!" they shout.

The basket settles on the ground,
Then Rupert hears a welcome sound.

It's Rupert's parents, bringing treats.
Mum's special ice-cream, drinks and sweets.

From one side of the carousel, you can see the whole Fair. From the other side, all you can see are trees and fields, until Rupert spots something unexpected flying overhead. A hot air balloon!

As soon as his ride is finished, Rupert goes to investigate. In the balloon are the Old Professor and Bodkin.

"We're here to give rides," smiles the Old Professor. "We couldn't miss out on the fun!"

"Oh yes, please!" cries Rupert.

He is so agog that the Professor agrees to take him up first.

But then an amazing noise of banging and trumpeting is heard. It's the ice-cream van, playing Rupert's jingle.

"You go and have an ice-cream first," says the Professor. "Ask your parents if they want to come up in the balloon."

The ice-cream jingle, playing loud,
Attracts a large and eager crowd.

An orange ice is just the thing
Before you go adventuring!

Then slowly up the basket flies,
His clever friend controls their rise.

The friends have risen very high
Into the blue and cloudless sky.

Rupert runs off towards the van. At the hatch, he can see Mum handing out ice-cream to eager children.

"Why don't you and Dad come up in the balloon?" he suggests.

"Oh, I don't think so," says Mum. "Who'd provide the ice-cream? You go and have fun."

Rupert gets himself a yummy orange lolly and licks it until his tongue tingles. Then he pockets the stick and runs back to the balloon.

The Old Professor is just bringing down a family of excited otters. As soon as they climb out, Rupert climbs in, and up they go!

Rupert waves to Dad, watching from the ice-cream van, and his friends who are waiting to go on the slide.

"You can see everything from up here!" he says.

But that isn't quite true. Rupert is looking down, and the Professor is checking the ropes, so that neither of them see the clouds gathering in the west.

"I think a storm is coming fast!
We'd best go down until it's passed."

A gust blows their balloon adrift!
The heavy anchor starts to lift.

Both Rupert and his old friend gasp,
And scrabble for some ropes to grasp.

And then they feel the anchor catch…
But only on the ice-cream hatch!

Fortunately, the Professor spots the storm before it hits them.

"Look at that," he says, pointing. "A storm's coming. I'd better get us down as quickly as I can."

But he isn't quite quick enough! A huge gust of wind hits the balloon before it has reached the earth. They hear the anchor tear out of its metal fixings with a horrible creak.

"Oh dear me!" pants the Professor. "Hang on!"

Rupert grabs the edge of the basket and hangs on for dear life. Below him the anchor is swinging wildly about on its rope. Bodkin ducks as it flies over his head

Then there is a loud CLANGGG!

"Oh good, the anchor's caught on something," gasps the Professor, who is struggling with the ropes.

But only Rupert can see what that something is!

"You'd better take a look," he tells his friend.

Rupert and the Ice-Cream Van

DAD'S ICE-CREAM VAN GOES FOR A RIDE

Now Rupert's left the storm behind,
There's trouble of another kind!

His mum and dad are being brave.
"We're fine down here!" they call, and wave.

"This isn't quite the ride I planned,"
The pilot says. "The van must land!"

"You'd better get down safely, too.
I'll rope you up and lower you."

The Old Professor is quite speechless as he looks down to see the ice-cream van sailing along below them, caught on the anchor. Mr Bear is craning out of the driver's window with a worried look on his face.

"I'm all right!" Rupert shouts down to him.

"Us too!" Dad calls back.

Nevertheless, this is not how things were supposed to work out.

"We need to get as much weight as possible into the van if we are to bring it in to land," says the Professor. "Shall I lower you down?"

Rupert is a little afraid, but he doesn't show it. He knows Mum will be worried, so he had better go down and reassure her.

"It'll be fun!" he grins.

So the Old Professor ropes him up as firmly and safely as possible, ready to be lowered over the edge of the basket.

RUPERT IS LOWERED TO HIS PARENTS

As Rupert's lowered, he can see
His parents waiting nervously.

Adventure's great, but Rupert's glad
To be safe back with Mum and Dad!

On hearing the Professor's scheme,
The Bears say "thank-you" with ice-cream!

The Old Professor waves a hand,
To indicate he'll try to land.

Rupert goes swinging down on the end of the rope. It's rather scary, but he can see Mum and Dad leaning out of the van hatch to grab him.

"All right, my lad, we'll catch you!" says Dad.

Rupert's parents grab hold of him and pull him into the flying van.

"My goodness me," says Mrs Bear, giving him a big hug. "Well, I suppose we're having a ride after all! But I think I'd rather be on the ground."

Rupert is inclined to agree.

"The Professor is going to find a place to land us," he tells his parents. "We just need to wait until we can find a suitable place."

"Excellent idea," says Mum, as Dad finishes untangling the rope from Rupert. "Here, I'll send him an ice-cream to keep his spirits up."

Rupert ties a basket to the rope he came down on. The Professor hauls it up and pulls out a lolly.

THE VAN IS LOWERED INTO A FIELD

The Bears have had enough of flight.
They want to find a landing site!

To have a chance of doing that
They need a field that's very flat.

The van is lowered to take a pass.
Its back wheels skim across the grass.

Just look at where they land instead –
A flimsy wooden jetty head.

The trouble with finding somewhere to land is that they are currently flying over woodland. Lowering the van here would leave it either in the top of one big tree, or sitting on a pile of broken saplings.

Neither idea appeals to the Professor so he goes sailing on looking for a nice flat field.

"There we are!" he shouts eventually. His words come down faintly to the Bear family in the van.

"Here we go," says Rupert bravely, holding on to

Mum's hand as she is looking rather worried. Dad has his eyes shut!

The back wheels of the van go THUNK on to the ground. But the grass is wet from the storm, and the van is moving fast, so instead of coming to rest it goes skidding back up into the air.

"Drat!" they hear the Old Professor shout.

The van drops again, but they've run out of field! They are coming down on an old jetty.

BUT MISSES!

The jetty groans, planks snap and smash.
The platform hits the river – SPLASH!

How Rupert and his parents laugh
To find they've made themselves a raft!

It's strange to see a two-tonne truck
Go paddling like a giant duck.

However, floating down a stream
Brings one more chance to sell ice-cream.

The jetty is only made of old rotten wood. As soon as the van hits it, there is a horrible groaning creak and the platform splits away from the supports.

The Bears get ready to scramble out of the windows, but there's no need. The ice-cream van hasn't sunk, it's started to float away down the river with the jetty underneath it as a raft!

"Well, well, well," says Dad in bemusement. "This must be the most adventurous ice-cream van ever."

Rupert laughs, and points at a passing boat. "Look, there's Sailor Sam!"

Sam is astonished to find Rupert floating down the river in a van. He says it must be the strangest ship he's ever seen, and then he buys an orange lolly.

"Why, the river is just the place to be selling ice-cream," says Mum, tidying the machines and boxes of supplies that were thrown about when the van was up in the air.

THE IMPS ENJOY SOME ICE-CREAM TOO

Before they've drifted very far,
The family spot the Squire's car.

Two worried friends are sat inside,
But they can't help; the gap's too wide.

A crafty imp comes swinging by
And grabs an ice while staying dry.

They pass ice-creams to several more,
But that won't help the Bears ashore!

The amazing flying ice-cream van has not gone unnoticed by the rest of Nutwood. The next time Rupert looks out of the window, he sees his friends Bill and Edward following in the Squire's car.

"What are you doing?" cries Bill with a slightly worried grin, while Edward waves.

"We landed on a jetty and it turned into a raft!" Rupert shouts back.

Then, they hear an excited chattering in the trees.

The Imps of Spring have come out of their caves and climbed up into the branches to see what all the commotion is about.

"Can we have some ice-cream?" they ask the Bears.

"Of course," says Rupert. "But I'll have to throw it over to you."

There's no need for that. First, one of the imps swings out on a vine and comes back clutching a cone, and soon all the others follow her example.

RUPERT HEADS OUT TO SEA

The Squire drives the best he can,
But how to reach the floating van?

And where the river meets the bay
The road bends off the other way!

The river widens gradually
And picks up speed towards the sea.

Then the river starts to flow faster, getting wider and wider.

"Can you find something to paddle with, and come in to the shore?" suggests Bill.

But before Rupert can think about this idea, the van reaches a bend in the river. The road goes one way, back inland, while the river heads out to sea.

"See you down on the beach!" shouts Rupert to his friends.

But as the van goes floating down to the bay, he really doesn't know how he's going to manage that.

Seagulls are crying overhead, and the air gets chillier as the Bears head towards the open water.

"I think we might have to swim back to shore," says Dad, eyeing the sea with some concern. "It could be rather rough out there."

"Oh please don't let's abandon the ice-cream van," begs Rupert. "I'm sure someone will help us!"

RUPERT IS SAVED FROM THE ROCKS

They're carried out beyond the bluff
And find the sea is rather rough.

They hear a nearby merboy shout,
"You're heading for a reef! Look out!"

"I'll help," the serpent booms, and blocks
The van from smashing on the rocks.

The merboy asks a magic trout
To take this rope and help them out.

Dad was right to be worried. As soon as the van floats out from between the protecting cliffs, the sea, which has been whipped up by the storm, turns out to be very rough. The Bears are tossed up and down, up and down, until they feel quite dizzy.

Fortunately, Rupert was right too. All the sea creatures come to the surface of the water to see this strange boat, and among them is a curious merboy, and a big, friendly sea serpent.

"You're floating on to the reef!" the merboy warns.

"Don't worry," booms the sea serpent. "I'll swim between you and the rocks."

Once the sea serpent is blocking off the dangerous current, Dad throws a rope to the merboy. He ties one end to the front of the raft, and gives the other to a huge fish who has come to see if she can help.

"It's nice having visitors, but I think you'll be happier on land!" the merboy smiles.

The trout sets off towards the beach,
But landfall is beyond her reach.

Now wavelets push them up the sand,
And soon the van is safe on land.

"Some fair!" says Rupert's dad. "Good grief…"
His friends come running in relief.

"It's all worked out," the good friends beam,
And then they go and eat ice-cream!

The fish is magical, and very strong. She pulls the van easily through the waves. The one thing she can't do is get right up to the beach. But fortunately the waves are strong enough here to carry the van the rest of the way to safety.

Finally, Rupert and his family are back on land!

"I wonder if the engine still goes?" muses Dad.

"Don't drive far," warns Mum. "I've had enough for one day!"

Luckily, the engine sputters into life with a bit of coaxing. Dad guides the van to a spot higher up on the beach, where he parks safely.

Rupert jumps out, and runs to see his friends, who have driven up to meet him. He tells them all about the merboy, the sea serpent and the magic fish.

"But are you all right?" asks Edward, to make sure.

Rupert's answer makes it clear: "Come on! Race you back to the van for ice-cream!"

JOIN THE DOTS

Going from 1 to 52, then starting again at A and going to W, join the dots to help Rupert and his dad put the finishing touches to their handsome vintage ice-cream van.

UNLOCK THE TREASURE

The Old Professor has found this locked box in a cupboard,
and can't remember what's inside. Could it be treasure?
Help Rupert and the Professor unscramble the locks, then check your answers below.

0 7 5

Example:
Reel A is less than 1
Reel B times Reel C = 35

Lock 1:
All the reels show
the same number.
The reels add up to 15.

Lock 2:
Reel A times Reel B = 1.
Reel C = Reel B + 8.

Lock 3:
Reel A is 2 times 3.
Reel B times Reel C = 21
Reel C is less than 6.

23

RUPERT'S BEANSTALK GAME

Rupert and his friends are going to see the Giant! The first one to the top of the beanstalk is the winner.

You will need a dice. Decide who will be Rupert, Clara, Tigerlily and Gregory (you can cut out the counters from the edge of the page, or use your own).

Then stand up and see who can jump the highest into the air! That person rolls first.

35
You eat a yummy bean and feel stronger!
GO FORWARD THREE PLACES.

36

34

33

22

23

24
Gregory gets overexcited and swings on the beanstalk. MISS A TURN IF YOU ARE GREGORY.

25

21
You accidentally step on the head of the person below you! GO FORWARD ONE PLACE, THEN MISS A TURN WHILE YOU APOLOGISE.

19
Tigerlily drops the flower from her hair. GO BACK TWO PLACES IF YOU ARE TIGERLILY.

18

17

20

5
A giant fly gives you a lift. MOVE FORWARD FOUR PLACES.

2

3
You find a good thick frond that you can climb quickly. GO FORWARD THREE PLACES.

4

Start
1

37
You need a rest from all this climbing. **MISS A TURN.**

38

39

Finish

30
The beanstalk grows one more tendril and Rupert goes up the wrong way. **GO BACK TWO PLACES IF YOU ARE RUPERT.**

31

32
A bluebottle flies into you. Ow! **MISS A TURN.**

29
A kind bee brings you some strengthening honey. **MOVE FORWARD TWO PLACES.**

26
A bird flies past and knocks everyone askew. **CHANGE PLACES WITH THE PLAYER FARTHEST BEHIND YOU.**

27

28

13
You use a leaf as a trampoline! **GO FORWARD ONE PLACE.**

15

14

12

16
The beanstalk flaps around in a gust of air. **MISS A TURN WHILE YOU HANG ON.**

9
Clara's whiskers get tangled in the leaves. **MISS A TURN IF YOU ARE CLARA.**

11
You help the person closest to you. **BOTH GO FORWARD THREE PLACES.**

7

6

8

10

RUPERT'S RIDDLES

Can you help Rupert solve the riddles that his brainy friend Bingo Pup has set for him?
The answer to each line of the riddles is a letter, and the eight letters form a word.

My first is in fixed but it's also in loose,
My second is found in both giant and goose.
My third is in twiggy but isn't in twig,
My fourth is the start of both Podgy and Pig.
My fifth is the start and the end of 'this text',
A word meaning 'me' is the sound that comes next.
My seventh is right in the middle of train,
My last is in knotty but also in plain.

| E | G | Y | P | T | I | A | N |

My first is in soup and it's also in pies,
My second's a word that you say in surprise.
My third is in scorn but it's also in greet,
My fourth's in the road and again in the street.
My fifth letter sounds like a round thing that sees,
My sixth is the start of distress and disease.
My seventh's in Algy and also in Pug
My eighth is in huge but it isn't in hug.

| P | O | R | R | I | d | g | E |

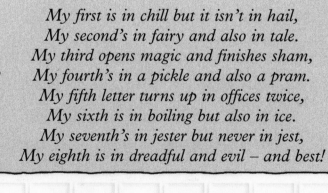

My first is in chill but it isn't in hail,
My second's in fairy and also in tale.
My third opens magic and finishes sham,
My fourth's in a pickle and also a pram.
My fifth letter turns up in offices twice,
My sixth is in boiling but also in ice.
My seventh's in jester but never in jest,
My eighth is in dreadful and evil – and best!

| C | A | M | P | F | I | R | E |

RUPERT

and the
Fairy-Tales

RUPERT READS HIS LIBRARY BOOK

"I wanted to go out and play,"
Sighs Rupert. "But I can't today!"

He settles down to read instead,
While Mum starts baking gingerbread.

The characters he reads about
First wave at him, then jump right out!

The pages riffle and produce
A wolf, three pigs, a boy, a goose…

Rupert is disappointed today. He was hoping to have a kickabout with his friends, but there's no hope of that in this weather. Grey rain is streaking out of the sky and splashing into the garden.

"Oh dear," says Mum, when she sees him looking sadly out of the window. "Why don't you read your library book instead?"

Rupert brightens up when he hears that idea. His new book of fairy-tales will be just the thing.

Rupert settles down to read, while the smell of gingerbread wafts in from the kitchen, where his mum is baking. But when he turns the page, something jumps out at him!

It's a gingerbread man. And he's not alone. A witch jumps out of the book, and three pigs, and a boy with a goose… They're going so fast Rupert can't work out what all of them are. But the last one looks rather scary. Rupert thinks it might be a wolf!

ALL THE PICTURES LEAVE THE BOOK

The creatures fling the front door wide
And head into the countryside.

Are any left? He takes a look,
But all the tales have fled their book!

So Rupert vaults the garden gate
And runs behind them, shouting: "Wait!"

They've pelted through the underbrush
And knocked down Podgy in their rush.

Rupert watches in astonishment as the strange figures fling the front door open and go charging outside. The sun is shining now too, which seems a bit odd, but Rupert is too busy to wonder about that.

He goes back to look at his book, and sees that all the pages are empty where they once had pictures.

It's hard to believe, but it seems the characters have jumped out of his book and run away.

Rupert realises he has to get them back!

The fairy-tale characters have run far ahead, but Rupert leaps over his garden gate and goes running into the fields, shouting: "Wait!"

But either the characters are out of earshot or they aren't listening.

The running figures disappear into the woods. Rupert comes puffing up to the edge of the trees, and almost falls over Podgy, who is lying in the undergrowth rubbing his head.

He checks that Podgy isn't hurt
Then follows footprints in the dirt.

He starts along a gloomy track
Still calling softly: "Please come back..."

As Rupert walks, the eerie sound
Of frightened weeping echoes round.

A little man with currant eyes!
"The big wolf chased us out..." he cries.

"Oh... ohhh," groans Podgy. "A crowd of strange people in funny costumes came barrelling past and knocked me over!" He stops and gives Rupert a look. "You think I'm making it up, don't you?" he accuses.

"No, I don't!" grins Rupert ruefully. "It really is very strange, but they're characters from my book, and I need to get them back. It's a library book!"

Rupert helps Podgy up, then starts down the path into the dark woods.

He calls softly, but nobody replies. But after a few minutes' walking he hears weeping nearby.

Sounds tend to echo and get louder in the dark forest, so the weeping sounds quite alarming until Rupert finds where it is coming from.

The little gingerbread man from his book is sitting on a rock with his face in his hands.

"The wolf chased us out of the book," he whimpers. "He wants to eat all the characters from every story!"

RUPERT FINDS THE GINGERBREAD MAN

For someone made of gingerbread,
It's safer up on Rupert's head.

The tiny man goes home for good,
It's just too scary in the wood.

So Rupert carries on, and sees
Three pigs beside a clump of trees.

But something gives the pigs a jolt.
They stare past Rupert, then they bolt.

"Well, that won't do," says Rupert kindly. "There's meant to be a wolf in Red Riding Hood's story, but not yours! I'll tell you what - you can ride on my head while we look for the others. You'll be safe up there."

The gingerbread man climbs up gratefully and nestles in Rupert's fur. But then they hear a long, shuddering howl, alarmingly close by.

"It's the wolf!" cries the gingerbread man. "I'm going home!"

With a flash and a rain of magic sparkles, he vanishes back into Rupert's book.

"Well, well," says Rupert to himself, not liking to think about the howl. "So it is possible to get them back into the book. If I can catch them."

He keeps walking down the path, until he spots three pigs hiding behind a stand of trees."

"Hullo!" he says. "I'm no wolf, I won't hurt you!" But the pigs stare past him in terror, then flee.

RUPERT IS CAUGHT BY THE WOLF

Soon Rupert finds he's lost the pigs,
And then he hears a crunch of twigs.

A strange, tall man in evening clothes,
With red eyes and a long, sharp nose.

A paw grabs Rupert by the throat.
It's Mr Wolf inside that coat!

He's left quite helpless by a tree.
The wolf will gobble him for tea!

"Don't be afraid!" Rupert calls after them. But really he knows it can't be him that has scared the pigs.

"I don't like this!" he thinks. "What's behind me?" Rupert turns around, and sees... a big, bad wolf!

"Hello," says Rupert, trying to be friendly.

But the wolf isn't interested in making friends. With one paw he grabs Rupert roughly by the arm, and with the other he takes a big coil of rope out of his inside jacket pocket.

Rupert looks nervously up at the wolf.

"What big teeth you have!" he says.

"All the better to eat you with," growls the wolf.

He grabs Rupert by the back of his jumper and drags him off to a clearing.

"I'll be back to gobble you up," promises the wolf. "I've some fairy-tales to capture first. I'll eat them all!"

Rupert is in rather a pickle. The wolf might be a storybook character, but he seems very real just now.

RUPERT IS RESCUED BY BILL

The woods around seem deathly still
Till Rupert hears a "Psst!" It's Bill!

"What luck!" says Rupert thankfully,
And soon the badger has him free.

The friends creep onwards through the wood
And soon they meet Red Riding Hood.

But then they hear some branches crack.
A squirrel warns them: "Trouble's back!"

Rupert wriggles, but it's no good. The ropes are very tight, and he can't get his hands near the knots.

"Psst!" he hears suddenly.

"Who's that?" asks Rupert. He hopes it's not some other evil fairy-tale character.

Then, Bill's friendly face appears from the bushes!

"Well, you are in a mess!" whispers Bill. But he wastes no more time before setting Rupert free.

Rupert explains what has happened.

"What a story," Bill chuckles. "I'll help, of course!"

"Hello," says a new voice. "What's going on?"

It's Red Riding Hood, in a bright hood and cloak.

"The wolf comes from your story," says Rupert urgently. "Perhaps you could help us capture him?"

"The wolf?" she wails. "But I got away from him!"

"I'm afraid he came after you!" says Bill. "In fact, he's after everybody now!"

"Ssh!" hisses a squirrel nearby. "He's back!"

RED RIDING HOOD RETURNS TO THE BOOK

*Red Riding Hood lets out a wail
And jumps straight back inside her tale.*

*She looks back out and gives a wave.
"I'm safe in here," she mouths. "Be brave!"*

*"Right," Rupert says. "That's two I've found.
The rest of them must be around!"*

*Just off the path, behind a stone,
A little boy is sat alone.*

Red Riding Hood doesn't want to hang around waiting for the wolf. In a fountain of sparkles, she vanishes back into Rupert's library book. When he turns to the page where her story starts, he sees her waving up at him from the paper.

"Sorry!" she mouths. "You'll have to be brave and catch the wolf!"

"Yes, we'd better!" says Rupert, though he wishes the characters would be more helpful.

Still, it's good to know that two of the fairy-tale people are back where they belong. Perhaps if Rupert can catch them all, the wolf will go back too.

"Is it all right to put him back in there with them?" wonders Rupert.

"Oh yes," Bill tells him. "The wolf gets his just desserts in the end. You read the story and see!"

"I hope I'll have the chance!" chuckles Rupert.

They run on, and spot someone sitting by the path.

RUPERT MEETS JACK AND HIS MAGIC BEANS

"Well, yes, I'm from your book. I'm Jack.
You needn't think I'm going back!"

While Rupert wonders what he means,
Sly Jack throws down some little beans.

Strange tendrils coil up from the grass,
And grab at Rupert as they pass.

The beanstalk hoists him way up high
Then grows straight on towards the sky.

The new character is wearing medieval costume.
"I'm Jack," he says, and seems friendly enough at
first. But he scowls when he sees Rupert's book.

"Oh no," he warns. "I'm not going back in there!"

"Shouldn't you go back to your story?" asks Bill.

"Not a chance. I'm the adventurous type, and I
like this new world. Ooh, look over there!"

Rupert and Bill look, and Jack throws a handful of
beans down where he has been pointing.

"Oh-oh!" shouts Bill, as a vine sprouts out of the
ground with amazing speed.

Rupert tries to jump aside, but it's too late. The
tendrils have wrapped around the friends' feet. Soon
Rupert and Bill are lifted into the air as the huge
beanstalk grows upwards.

"Bye-bye!" says Jack, waving cheekily.

"I'll be back!" Rupert promises. But promising is
all he can do at the moment!

RUPERT AND BILL ON THE BEANSTALK

The friends head up towards a shroud
Of heavy, swirling, clinging cloud.

Eventually the tendrils stop.
They've reached a castle at the top.

At least it seems the magic stalk
Has dropped them somewhere safe to walk.

"I wonder who could live up here?"
Says Rupert, swallowing his fear.

The beanstalk carries on growing upwards so fast that Rupert and Bill only have time to exchange a few words, mostly "help!" and "oh dear!", before they are lifted right up into the clouds.

"These clouds seem very thick," pants Bill, and Rupert thinks he is right.

In fact, when the beanstalk reaches the top of the clouds and suddenly stops growing, the friends find they can walk safely on the white surface.

"It's solid," Rupert assures Bill, who is following him. "Quite bouncy, in fact. Whee!"

And Rupert jumps up into the air to amuse his friend, though really he's feeling rather worried.

Looming over everything up here is a huge castle.

"That must belong to the fairy-tale giant," says Bill.

"I wish I'd had time to read the book!" says Rupert. "Is the giant friendly?"

Bill bites his lip, and says: "Not to Jack, he's not."

RUPERT AND THE GIANT

The friends just push the door ajar.
It weighs too much to give that far.

A cautious Rupert takes a peek
And winces as the hinges squeak.

They've hardly got inside the door
When Rupert's lifted off the floor.

But soon the giant sets him free
And listens sympathetically.

Still, there's nowhere to go except into the castle. Rupert bravely knocks, but gets no answer. So he pushes the huge, weighty door.

The door will only open a crack, but it's enough for Rupert to squeeze inside.

"Hello...?" he tries cautiously.

"FEE, FI, FO, FUM!" comes a terrible voice from overhead. Rupert is grabbed by his sweater and hoisted into the air!

"I SMELL THE BLOOD OF..." starts the giant, then pauses. "HMM," he says, putting Rupert down on his enormous table and lifting up Bill to join him.

"YOU'RE NOT THAT SCALLYWAG JACK," he says, still booming, but sounding much less scary.

"No, we're not," says Rupert. "Jack tricked us into getting carried up here." And he tells the giant all about the beanstalk.

"TYPICAL OF JACK!" grumbles the giant.

"See what this tale should be about?
It's you! Somehow you've fallen out."

"The wolf's behind this, that's my guess,"
The giant rumbles. "What a mess!"

"This goose will follow my command
And fly you safely back to land."

They settle on the golden goose,
And then the giant turns it loose.

Rupert shows the giant his book of fairy-tales.

"This is where you belong," he explains. "But somehow the big bad wolf from another story found a way out, and everything seems to have leaked. Some of the characters have gone back, but Jack refuses."

"DEARIE ME," booms the giant. "WE CAN'T HAVE THAT JACK CAUSING TROUBLE IN YOUR WORLD AS WELL AS MINE. WE'LL ALL HAVE TO GO BACK INTO THE BOOK."

"The trouble is, most of the characters are down in the forest, and we are stranded up here," says Rupert.

"DON'T WORRY ABOUT THAT," the giant reassures him. "MY GOLDEN GOOSE WILL CARRY YOU SAFELY BACK TO EARTH."

He sets the two friends on the goose's back, and she flies out of the castle window, heading downwards.

"Thank you!" Rupert and Bill call to the giant. "We'll tell Jack to leave you alone!"

THE GOLDEN GOOSE RETURNS TO THE BOOK

The goose shoots Jack a beady glare
As if to say: "You help this bear!"

She drops her riders in the glade
Then slowly starts to blur and fade.

The goose shrinks down to Rupert's hand
And takes her place in story land.

When Rupert looks, he's pleased to see
The goose wink back quite happily.

Jack is rather surprised to see Rupert and Bill come flying back on a giant goose. He takes a few steps back when the goose gives him a beady glare, just as if to say, "You'd better watch out!"

"What were you going to do to the giant?" Rupert asks Jack.

"Steal his magic harp and his goose's golden eggs," says Jack sheepishly, scuffing the ground.

"Just because he's a giant?" asks Rupert.

"Giants are evil!" says Jack.

"Not this one!" says Bill. "He just saved us. I think you'd better help us out as an apology."

"Oh, all right," Jack looks sulky, but clearly he feels guilty, too.

The goose smiles when she hears all this. Then she starts to turn faint, and shrink into the air above Rupert's book. When he looks at the pictures, he sees the goose is safely back home, and the giant too!

RUPERT AND THE THREE BEARS' COTTAGE

A trail of breadcrumbs seems to say
More characters have passed this way.

They keep their eyes fixed on the grass.
A shadow watches as they pass.

They spot a cottage down the hill.
"They must have gone in there," says Bill.

"Hello?" the three companions call
As Rupert steps inside the hall.

Now Jack has agreed to help them, Rupert feels their chances of catching everyone are a little better.

Soon he spots some breadcrumbs on the ground.

"That probably means Hansel and Gretel," says Bill. "They tried to use a trail of breadcrumbs to stop them getting lost in the woods. But it didn't work because the crumbs got eaten!"

Sure enough, a little bird hops up and starts eating the crumbs.

So the friends just have to go on down the path.

"I feel like we're being watched," murmurs Bill, and Rupert knows what he means.

The path leads down a hill towards a little cottage.

"Oh no!" groans Bill. "This is too good to be true. It must be the witch's house!"

"Maybe she's friendly, like the giant," says Rupert.

Once again, he finds himself peering around a strange door.

RUPERT AND GOLDILOCKS

A pudgy child in bows and lace
Is scoffing porridge down apace.

When Rupert tries a subtle cough,
The frightened Goldilocks runs off.

"I feel so bad," she sobs. "I stole
A bear cub's porridge from his bowl!"

They hear a growling from the glade.
"I'm going!" Goldie squeaks, afraid.

But the person they see inside isn't a witch. It's a chubby little girl, scoffing porridge.

"The fairy-tales are all mixed up," whispers Bill. "That's Goldilocks!"

When Goldilocks catches sight of Rupert, she screams, pushes him away and runs off.

"A bear!" she shrieks.

"Yes, but I'm a nice bear!" protests Rupert, not sure if Goldilocks is a very nice girl.

Rupert and Bill run after her, and find her sobbing in the woods.

"I'm sorry," she cries. "It just smelled so good..."

"What did?" asks Rupert, bewildered.

"In her story, she crept into some bears' house, and stole the baby's porridge," explains Bill.

"Ah!" Rupert smiles. "This book..." he starts.

But then they hear a terrible howl.

"You'll have to excuse me!" says Goldilocks.

GOLDILOCKS RETURNS TO THE BOOK

She fades from vision in a haze
Of sparkly mist and magic rays.

She smiles at him from story land,
Then waves a rather sticky hand.

The wolf is back! They run inside
A curious house of sweets to hide.

Some characters are in here too.
They say: "We're hiding, just like you!"

With a *flash, bang, sparkle!* Goldilocks is back inside her story. She gives Rupert a relieved smile, but Rupert has no time to be relieved himself. The wolf is coming, crashing his way through the undergrowth.

Rupert, Bill and Jack run blindly on, until they come to a house that is very strange indeed. All the walls and even the roof are made of sweets.

"This is definitely the witch's house!" pants Bill. "It's in the story of Hansel and Gretel!"

Maybe so, but nobody wants to stay outside with a hungry wolf. The boys slam the door behind them, and Rupert leans against it.

"Phew!" he says, then has a look around him.

Staring back at him are all the missing fairy-tale characters, including the witch.

"Don't you hurt Hansel and Gretel!" Bill warns the old crone.

"I won't," she says. "If you save me from the wolf!"

THE WOLF HUFFS AND PUFFS

It's no use hiding any more –
The wolf is snuffling at the door!

The wolf comes right up close, and howls!
"I'll blow your house right down," he growls.

And when he starts to huff and puff,
The cottage walls aren't strong enough!

Poor Rupert flies up in a whirl.
The room around him starts to swirl.

"All right!" agrees Rupert. But he's not sure what he can do. The wolf is scrabbling at the door now.

One of the pigs lets out a frightened squeal.

"Little pig, little pig, let me in!" growls the wolf.

"Not by the hair on my chinny chin chin!" squeaks the pig.

"This is no good," whispers Bill. "In the fairy-tale, the wolf blows the pig's stick house down. I don't suppose a house of sweets will fare much better."

Bill is right!

"Then I'll huff and I'll puff and I'll blow your house down!" snarls the wolf.

And that is just what he does. The liquorice and toffee walls give way, and everyone falls together. People start yelling, and everything spins very fast. Rupert flies up in the air and turns head over heels until he doesn't know which way is up or where he is any more.

WHERE DID THESE BEANS COME FROM?

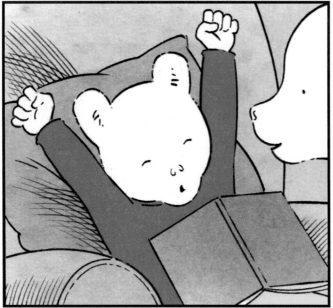

A voice says: "Wake up, little bear!"
And Rupert finds he's in his chair.

He shakes himself, stands up, and blinks.
"That must have been a dream," he thinks.

Can Dad explain what all this means?
Especially the pile of beans!

His dad decides to plant the lot,
But Rupert says he'd better not!

Then, suddenly, everything is quiet.

Rupert opens his eyes, and finds that he is sitting in the armchair where all this started.

"Wake up, little bear!" his mum is saying, with a gentle smile.

Rupert stands up and blinks hard. He shakes himself, pinches himself and looks at his book. All the pictures are in place.

"So, all that was a dream!" he exclaims to himself.

But then he feels some little hard lumps in his pocket. It's a handful of beans!

"What's going on here?" he wonders. "I obviously didn't imagine these."

Rupert goes to ask his dad what he thinks.

But Dad doesn't listen properly. He just exclaims over the beans: "These will grow well in the garden."

And off he goes to plant them. Rupert will have to explain why this is not a good idea!

RUPERT'S SHADOW ANIMALS

Go into a dark room and set up a direct light, such as a torch, to shine against a blank wall. Then copy these hand movements to make pictures of your favourite characters magically appear.

Algy Pug

Edward Trunk

Wise Old Goat

Golden Goose

RUPERT'S COLOURING

SPOT THE DIFFERENCE

The pictures below look the same, but there are 10 differences in picture 2.
Can you spot them all?

①

②

THE HISTORY OF RUPERT BEAR

Rupert has been appearing in newspapers and annuals for over 80 years. Your mum and dad probably remember him from their childhood – and your grandma and grandad, too! Here's the brief story of how Rupert became the special bear we know today.

Mary Tourtel's Rupert (1920 to 1935)

Rupert was first created in 1920 by an artist called Mary Tourtel. The *Daily Express* newspaper needed a cartoon strip that would appeal to young readers, and outdo Teddy Tail, a character in a rival publication. Nobody knew then quite how successful Rupert was going to be!

Early Rupert has a blue shirt and white check trousers, but he's clearly recognisable as his later self. A lot of his best friends, such as Bill Badger and Edward Trunk, also date back to the 1920s.

Mary continued drawing Rupert until 1935, when health troubles led to the job being taken over by Alfred Bestall.

Alfred Bestall's Rupert (1935 to 1965)

Alfred Bestall, who drew over 270 strips, is the most famous of the Rupert artists. He introduced more magic into the Rupert stories, and created much of the Nutwood world we recognise now, from devising characters such as Bingo to setting the rule that Rupert was always to have exactly six stripes on his trousers, so he would look consistent!

Bestall's Rupert is a little more cuddly than Mary Tourtel's original, who looked more like a real bear. But his brave and helpful personality is just the same.

Some of Bestall's work has been reissued in the form of treasuries and albums, bringing it to today's audience.

John Harrold's Rupert (mid-1970s to mid-1990s)

When Alfred Bestall retired as sole Rupert artist, there was a long period when the strip was drawn by various different illustrators. John Harrold emerged as clearly the best of the bunch.

John worked with talented colourists, making Nutwood into a fresh, bright world and peopling it with friends old and new. Newspaper deadlines were tight, and sometimes John stayed up until 5am to draw panels, because there was too much noise for him to concentrate in the daytime.

John's work featured in the Rupert Annual until 2007 and can now be seen in *The Adventures of Rupert* story collection.

Stuart Trotter's Rupert (2008 - ongoing)

Until recently, Rupert stories had not been drawn for some time, meaning that the Annual reprinted classic stories. But now Stuart Trotter has taken up the pencil.

Stuart is a lifelong Rupert fan, who grew up reading Alfred Bestall's work. He describes the job of Rupert artist as 'a dream come true'. Like Bestall, he thinks up storylines for the Annual as well as drawing and colouring the artwork.

Stuart's Rupert is a tribute to the Bestall strips he grew up with, but his drawings also have a freshness all of their own.

Almost 90 years on from his birth, Rupert is going strong!

If you have ideas about what you'd like to see in future Rupert Annuals, why not answer the survey below and post it to us?

RUPERT BEAR READERSHIP SURVEY

To enter our free prize draw, fill out this survey online at **www.egmont.co.uk/rupertbearsurvey** or photocopy and send to: **Rupert Bear Readership Survey, Egmont UK Ltd. 239 Kensington High Street, London W8 6SA**. Entries are limited to one per household, no purchase necessary.

ABOUT RUPERT BEAR

❶ This Annual contains stories, puzzles and craft-making. Tick to indicate how much do you enjoy each kind of activity.

	REALLY LIKE	LIKE	DON'T LIKE
Stories	☐	☐	☐
Puzzles	☐	☐	☐
Crafts	☐	☐	☐

❷ Which of the following are you most attracted to when you are reading?

Pictures	☐	Headings	☐
Rhymes	☐	Story	☐

❸ Apart from Rupert Bear himself, who are your favourite characters? Please rank your top 10 in order with 1 being the highest.

Algy Pug	☐	Bill Badger	☐
Bingo Pup	☐	Clara Cat	☐
Edward Trunk	☐	Ottoline Otter	☐
Podgy Pig	☐	Tigerlily	☐
Gregory Guineapig	☐		
Other:			

❹ From the following list, circle the five words that best describe what you like about Rupert Bear:

fun nostalgia adventure excitement learning friendship nature magic fantasy storytelling pictures

❺ Who is your favourite Rupert Bear artist?

Mary Tourtel	☐	Alfred Bestall	☐
John Harrold	☐	Stuart Trotter	☐
Don't know	☐		

❻ What would you like to see in future Rupert Bear Annuals?

....
....
....
....
....
....
....

ABOUT YOU

❶ Have you purchased this annual for:

Yourself	☐	Your child	☐
Your grandchild	☐	Other:	

❷ Buyer's age:

Under 18	☐	18-24	☐	25-33	☐
34-42	☐	43-52	☐	53-65	☐
65+	☐				

❸ Reader's age:

0-3	☐	4-6	☐	7-10	☐
11-13	☐	14-17	☐	18-24	☐
25-33	☐	34-42	☐	43-52	☐
53-65	☐	65+	☐		

❹ Where do you prefer to buy your books?

Online	☐	Book shop	☐
Mail order	☐	Book club	☐
Other high street retailer (please specify)			

Fan's name: ....

Address: ....

Postcode: .... Date of birth: ....

(If applicable) Name of parent / guardian: ....

(If applicable) Email for parent / guardian: ....

RUPERT'S WORDSEARCH

The fairy-tale characters and objects have hidden again, this time in a word grid!
Can you find all the characters and objects?
Names can read up, down, sideways and diagonally.

```
D K E Y J R X M V H T T N
J O S N A S C P A I S N I
S R O I C U N N E K A A C
Z G O H K B S A C F H I R
F T G Y G E A O E C Z G F
E W N W L N L S T B X V K
J J E X O I I I K A A C Y
Q I D Q D L W D N E E A J
D V L L E Q F R I N T S L
V G O K E L E T E R G T Y
I G G G S L R S V Q D L X
B E A N S T A L K G F E X
P I G S X X H Q A Y F Z R
```

BASKET

CASTLE

JACK

BEANS

GIANT

PIGS

BEANSTALK

GOLDEN GOOSE

RED RIDING HOOD

GOLDILOCKS

WITCH

GRETEL

WOLF

HANSEL

50

RUPERT

and the
Branch Line

RUPERT HEARS OF THE SPECIAL TRAIN

Dad reads the news while Rupert plays.
"An exhibition's on," he says.

"A thousand relics from a crypt
Beneath the sands of old Egypt!"

"It's coming in by rail tonight.
The train will be a gorgeous sight!"

"I want to see it! Can I camp?
As getting there takes two hours' tramp..."

One afternoon, Rupert plays with his train set while his Dad looks through the newspaper.

Dad reads out the best articles, so Rupert can hear.

"Listen to this!" says Dad. "Nutchester will be hosting an exhibition of Egyptian treasure, including a mysterious prophecy stone from the pyramid tomb of Bearameses the Pharaoh. The exhibits will arrive at first light tomorrow, on a special Egyptian train."

"Why so early?" asks Rupert.

"It's because the relics are so valuable," explains Dad. "The authorities need to clear the line before the train can come through."

Rupert thinks the exhibition sounds interesting, but the train sounds even better!

"I really want to see it!" he says.

Rupert goes to ask his mum if he can take some friends and camp by the railway line that leads to Nutchester, to be sure of seeing the train.

RUPERT AND HIS FRIENDS SET OFF

*He gets permission from his mum
And asks some friends if they can come.*

*Before they're far along the way
Old Growler calls behind them: "Hey!"*

*"You'd best be careful, camping out.
There's storms and funny men about."*

*The friends agree, but persevere.
It's hard to think of danger here.*

Mum says yes, so Rupert goes to see who wants to join a camping trip. Edward Trunk wants to come, and so does Clara Cat. Clara has just moved to Nutwood from Nutchester, and really enjoys having the chance to go on long country rambles.

All three go home to fetch their camping things, then meet up again and set off towards the railway.

They haven't got very far when they hear a shout from behind them. It's PC Growler.

They wait for the policeman to catch up with them.

"Going camping, are we?" he says with a smile. "Well, mind how you go. There's a storm forecast. What's more, I've had reports of some strange men wandering around these woods."

"We'll be careful," promises Rupert, but he doesn't feel terribly worried about the weather or anything else. On a lovely day like this, who could?

The friends hitch up their packs, and stroll on.

THEY FIND THE PERFECT SPOT

A trail of smoke across the sky
Must mean a train will soon come by.

Toot toot! The engine lets off steam.
Its polished wheels and paintwork gleam.

They haven't put the tents up yet.
They'd better, as it might turn wet.

Strong Edward gathers logs to burn.
The tents are up by his return.

After a couple of hours of walking, the friends reach the railway line that takes trains into Nutchester. In the distance is a line of smoke, that tells them a train will be coming soon.

All three children lean against the fence to watch the train go past. It's spectacular, with its gleaming metal and polished paintwork, and its handsome funnel that sends out huge gouts of steam. Everything shakes as it rushes by!

Once the train is gone, the friends notice that there are black clouds in the sky as well as steam.

"We'd better put the tents up before we get wet!" says Rupert.

They search through the trees until they find a handy glade to camp in. Then Edward goes off to get wood for a cooking fire while Rupert and Clara assemble the tents. They have to try a couple of times to get them to stay up!

RUPERT HEARS AN ALARMING ROAR

"Ssh!" Clara hisses. "Who's that tramp?"
A man goes striding past their camp.

They talk about the man at tea.
"A crook!" says Edward. "Bound to be!"

But Rupert thinks that's rather steep,
And soon he settles down to sleep.

He's woken in the dead of night
By fearsome roars and blinding light!

By the time Edward comes back with the wood, the storm clouds have passed by without raining at all.

"Ssh!" hisses Clara suddenly.

The boys freeze. They can hear something too. It's a man, stomping through the undergrowth! But they stay very still, and he goes right past without seeing them.

The friends wait a long time to be sure he's gone, then they make their tea.

"I bet that was one of the crooks!" says Edward.

But Rupert and Clara are feeling relaxed and comfortable after a tasty dinner. They tell Edward not to be silly, because it was probably just a tramp.

Rupert sets his alarm clock to wake him in time for the train, then snuggles into his sleeping bag for the night. Soon he is fast asleep.

But not for long! It seems only a moment before he's startled awake by a horrible screeching roar, and a light as bright as day.

RUPERT FINDS THE BRANCH LINE

The stormy noises quickly fade
And night flows back into the glade.

The friends unearth a disused line
In bushes down a steep decline.

And far off, at the other end,
Some train lights vanish round a bend.

"Oh my," breathes Rupert when he sees
A crumbling station through the trees.

While Rupert scrambles out of his tent, the noise dies away and the lights fade. He sees that the others are up too, and are standing around looking amazed.

"That wasn't a storm," says Clara.

"I thought it was train brakes!" says Edward. "But the sound didn't come from the main line."

"Well, we'll have to investigate!" decides Rupert.

He leads his friends down a steep slope. There, overhung by bushes, they find some rusty tracks.

"It's a disused branch line!" Rupert realises.

They are just in time to see the lights of the train disappearing slowly around a bend.

"It's stopping," says Clara. "Shall we go and see?"

"Well, I certainly can't go straight back to sleep after all that!" grins Rupert. "Come on!"

They creep along until they see that the train has stopped at an old station. As they watch, the station lights come on and the chimney starts to smoke.

RUPERT AND EDWARD ARE CAUGHT

*The cooling pistons hiss and creak
As Rupert goes to take a peek.*

*"Take care!" warns Clara from the wood.
"I'm sure all this can mean no good."*

*"We'll get that train of artefacts!
We've switched the points to use these tracks."*

*The friends are listening in so hard
They miss the footsteps in the yard!*

Rupert and Edward decide to examine the train.

"Be careful," warns Clara. "I think Edward must have been right after all. Something odd's going on."

Rupert nods.

"Then we're going to find out what it is!" he says. motioning to the others to follow him towards the windows of the station house.

The friends steal up to the window and listen to the conversation of the men inside.

"We're all set, lads," a harsh voice is saying. "Mick's changed the points, so the special train will come down our line. Fred and me will handle the driver, then we take off with the treasure!"

The friends listen open-mouthed.

"We have to get help!" whispers Edward.

Too late! One of the gang has spotted them.

"What have we here?" the man snarls, stepping up behind them and lifting Edward by his collar.

RUPERT AND EDWARD ARE TIED UP

But Clara hides behind a crate.
She winks to Rupert, mouthing: "Wait!"

"We'll lock these silly kids away
Until we're gone," the ruffians say.

"You nosy brats will be quite snug
In this here cupboard," smirks the thug.

One broken window lights the place
And through it they see Clara's face!

But the thug hasn't noticed Clara! She dives smoothly behind a crate and watches in dismay as her friends are dragged off.

"Wait!" she mouths to them. "I'll get you out!"

Rupert and Edward are taken to the gang leader.

"Horrible kids," he says, scowling at them. "Stick 'em in a cupboard. Someone will find them after we're long gone. Probably." He grins unpleasantly.

One of the henchmen ties the boys up.

"You'll be safe in here," he grins, shoving them into a cupboard and locking the door behind him.

The cupboard is cold and dingy. The only light comes from a glassless window overhead.

"Fancy a stroll?" says Clara's voice. The boys look up to see a familiar face peering in at them.

"I'll say!" exclaims Rupert.

Clara scrambles inside. Soon the boys are untied and climbing out to freedom.

She helps them get out through the hole
Then goes to find a police patrol.

The boys go running down the track
To find the points and turn them back.

If they can push this lever down
The train will rush straight on to town.

"Ssh!" Rupert whispers. "Help me quick!
I think the men have sussed our trick!"

As soon as they are safely away, Rupert comes up with a plan.

"Clara, you run into Nutchester and raise the alarm. Edward and I will go and change the points so the train won't come down the branch line!"

Clara runs back the way they came in, while the boys follow the tracks towards the main line. It's not long before they find the points the men talked about.

Rupert looks at the huge lever.

"It's pretty obvious how it works," he decides. "You just push it, and a bit of the track moves to guide the train in the right direction. But it looks terribly big and heavy."

"Let me have a go," says Edward.

Then, the boys freeze. Angry voices and footsteps are coming up the branch line behind them.

"Quick," whispers Rupert, and the boys both push on the lever together.

RUPERT AND EDWARD CHANGE THE POINTS

The points are changed, but now they hear
The heavy footsteps very near.

Although the men will put things back,
The boys can't stay beside the track.

The points are set to 'turn' again.
So now the gang will get the train!

The train goes puffing to its doom
While Rupert has to watch in gloom.

The lever groans... and sticks... and groans... and sticks again. It takes several seconds for them to edge it into position.

"Phew!" Edward pants triumphantly.

The points clank into place, and the boys flee into the safety of the bushes.

Not a moment too soon. Two burly men come tramping down the branch line, flashing a torch to look for the lever.

"Dratted kids," grumbles one of them. "I bet they've changed the points."

"They have, too," says his companion.

"Not to worry," grins the first man as they heave the lever back into position. "I can hear the train now. We'll be long gone by the time the police get here."

Sure enough, the special train comes rumbling up. It's a spectacular sight, but that's no comfort to Rupert and Edward now.

FAMILIAR FACES ON THE TRAIN

But look! The friends bite back a yell.
Their back-up plan is working well!

The squeals of nearby brakes suggest
The ambushed train has come to rest.

Old Growler soon arrests the mob;
The driver helps him do the job.

"These thugs thought I was off their trail,"
Says Growler. "Now they're off to jail!"

"Job done! Let's go and help the others!" growls one of the thugs, and they head back to the station.

The boys groan as the train chuffs past, heading down the branch line.

Then Rupert glimpses some familiar faces in one of the carriages.

"Clara made it!" he exclaims.

At once the boys run off towards the station house. They arrive to hear angry voices from inside.

They burst in at the main door to find PC Growler and the train driver tying up the villains.

"Well, well," says Growler, turning to Rupert and his friends when he's finished with the gang. "Until Clara came running up, I was stumped. I'd gone to Nutchester, thinking the ruffians would be trying to steal the treasure there! If it wasn't for you, I'd still be there, wondering why the train hadn't come."

"You're welcome!" says Rupert.

THE MAYOR THANKS THE FRIENDS

*The train chuffs off Nutchester-ward
With Rupert and his friends aboard.*

*The friends are asked to see the Mayor,
Who's heard about the whole affair.*

*"You children foiled a dreadful crime
By reaching Growler just in time."*

*The Mayor congratulates the three
And treats them to a fine cream tea.*

The friends collect their camping gear while Growler and the driver bundle the villains on to the train. Then they all set off for Nutchester.

Word has got around, and people are waiting for them at the station. Some Nutchester police have come to take charge of the criminals, and they bring the news that the Mayor himself wants to welcome Rupert and his friends, and thank them for helping to catch the gang.

The Mayor tells the friends how grateful he is.

"The relics are priceless and very mysterious," he says. "Scholars are still studying the carved stone writing. It would have been a catastrophe if the artefacts were stolen before they are even understood!"

As a thank-you, he treats all three of them to a gorgeous cream tea at Nutchester's finest tea shop.

Clara licks the cream from her whiskers, and Edward uses his trunk to slurp jam off his tusks!

Then Rupert heads back home again
To tell the story of the train.

"Our exhibition starts," reads Mum,
"Tomorrow afternoon. Please come."

But when the friends arrive, their host
Just stares as if he's seen a ghost.

There, chiselled into stone, they see
Fulfilment of a prophecy!

That afternoon, Rupert gets the train back to Nutwood, then hurries down the lane to see his parents and tell them all about his adventures.

He's got a letter from the Egyptian experts who are running the exhibition. Mum opens it for him.

"It's an invitation for all three of you to attend the grand opening tomorrow," she says.

So the next day, Rupert, Clara and Edward turn up at the appointed time and introduce themselves.

However, the Egyptian expert who greets them doesn't seem to be very talkative. He just keeps staring.

"Is something wrong?" asks Rupert politely.

"No... that is, I think we've solved the prophecy!" stutters the man. "Bearameses predicted 'a steaming metal beast', a great rescue and... well, come and see!"

He takes the friends to see one of the stone tablets. Carved among the Egyptian symbols are three figures with very familiar faces – their own!

RUPERT'S ORIGAMI

To create your own origami pyramid, start with a square of paper...

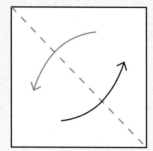

1. Fold and unfold.

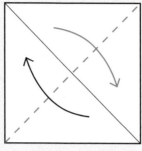

2. Fold and unfold.

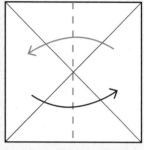

3. Fold and unfold.

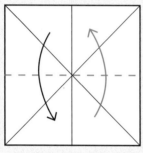

4. Fold and unfold.
Filp over the paper.

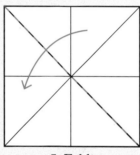

5. Fold.

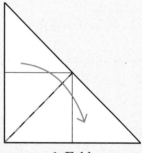

6. Fold.

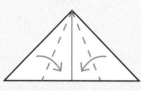

7. Fold the edges
to the middle.
Your shape should
now look like this. →
Crease well and unfold.

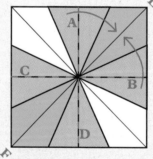

8. Fold lines A and B inwards and
over towards eachother.

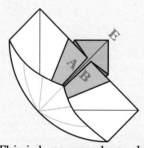

9. This is how your shape should
look now. You can stick it in
place if you wish.

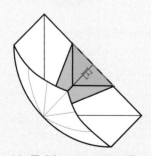

10. Fold over corner E.
Repeat these two steps with
folds C and D, and corner F.
This may be tricky as your
shape is now three-dimensional!

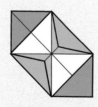

11. From underneath, your shape
should look like this. Now fold
the last two points under.
Stick in place if you wish.

12. WELL DONE!
Now you can decorate your
pyramid with Egyptian-style
drawings of Rupert and his friends,
just like those in the story!

RUPERT'S ANAGRAMS

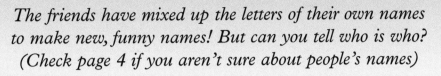

*The friends have mixed up the letters of their own names
to make new, funny names! But can you tell who is who?
(Check page 4 if you aren't sure about people's names)*

1. **Dud Krantwer** ....

2. **Blard Bilge** ....

3. **Cal Tacra** ....

4. **Lyap Ugg** ....

5. **Iggy Roger Unagipe** ....

6. **Peter Brura** ....

What funny words can you make from the letters in your name?

....

....

....

....

....

CLARA'S MAZE

Clara doesn't know her way around Nutwood yet! Can you help her find the way through the village to her new house? Remember you can go over or under the bridges, but not jump on or off them.

Answer:

RUPERT'S MEMORY TEST

Try this memory test only when you have read the whole annual.
Each of the pictures below is taken from one of the stories you have seen in this book.
Look carefully at them, then see if you can answer the questions.

1 Why has Podgy got a sore head?

2 What is Sailor Sam doing?

3 What is Rupert's dad reading about?

4 Who lives behind this door?

5 Who tied Rupert up?

6 What is in this box?

7 What does Rupert do when he can't go out?

8 What does this lever do?

9 Why is Clara hiding?

10 Who does the merboy hand this rope to?

11 Whose seeds grow into this giant vine?

12 Why has Edward gathered this wood?

13 What is Rupert waving at?

14 What is Mrs Bear making?

15 Who lives here?

16 Why is this pig running away?

Answers: 1 – the fairy-tale characters have knocked him over; 2 – buying an ice-cream from Rupert while he sails down the river; 3 – the Egyptian exhibition; 4 – the giant; 5 – the big, bad wolf; 6 – the jingle for the ice-cream van; 7 – he reads his library book of fairy-tales; 8 – it changes the points on the railway line; 9 – the train thieves have captured Rupert and Edward; 10 – the magic trout; 11 – Jack's; 12 – to make a camp fire; 13 – the Old Professor in his balloon; 14 – ice-cream; 15 – the Old Professor and Bodkin; 16 – he's heard the wolf coming.

67